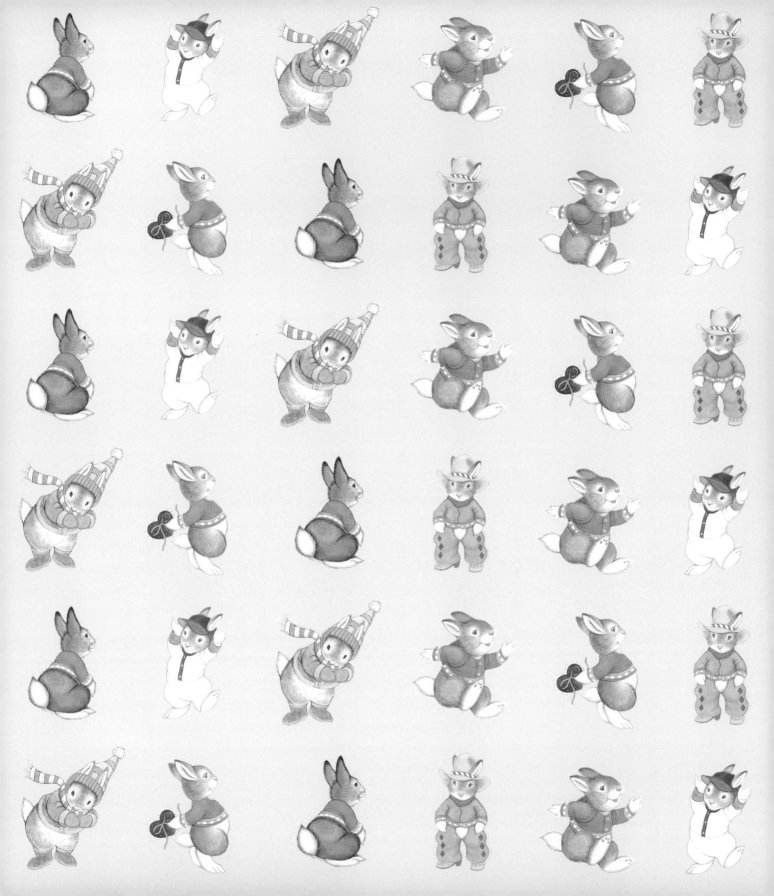

波波唸翻天系列 5

波波的下雪天

Justine Korman　著

Lucinda McQueen　繪

本局編輯部　譯

三民書局

For Monkey Boy,
who makes every day fun!
—J.K.

獻給每一天都充滿歡樂的小淘氣

—J.K.

For Kaylee and Jamie,
who always enjoy their snowy days
Love, Lucy

獻給喜歡下雪天的凱利和潔美
愛你們的露西

Published by Troll Associates, Inc.

One morning, Hopper woke up to a winter wonderland. But was the **grumpy** bunny happy? Of course not!

"**Boots** and **bother**," Hopper **grumbled**. He hated all the **fuss** of snow. And most of all, Hopper hated **shoveling**!

一天清晨，波波醒來發覺外面是一片冬日的雪景仙境。但這隻愛抱怨的兔子會因此而開心嗎？那可不！

「穿靴子真麻煩！」波波嘀嘀咕咕地抱怨著。他討厭下雪帶來的不便，尤其是，波波好討厭鏟雪。

While he ate breakfast, Hopper listened to the radio:
"**Due to** last night's storm, the following schools will be closed:
Bitty Bunny Preschool, Easter Bunny Elementary School..."

The grumpy bunny **sighed** with **relief**. At least he wouldn't have to go to school and be **pestered** by a **bunch** of excited kinderbunnies.

波波一邊吃早餐，一邊聽收音機，「由於昨晚暴風雪的影響，以下播報的幾所學校今天不上課：小兔寶寶幼幼班、復活節兔寶寶小學……」這隻愛抱怨的兔子鬆了一口氣，至少他不必到學校去，被一群興奮的小兔崽子擾得心煩。

Hopper pulled on his coat, boots, hat, **scarf**, and **mittens**.
"What a lot of stuff to wear," he complained. "Once I get all this
shoveling done, I'll come inside and have a nice, quiet day at home."

波波穿上外套、靴子、戴上帽子、圍巾及連指手套。「要穿這麼多雜七雜八的東西，」他
抱怨著。「只要一把雪鏟完，我就要進屋裡度過悠閒、平靜的一天。」

But as soon as the grumpy bunny stepped outside, he was **surrounded** by snow-happy kinderbunnies.

Little Muffin laughed. "Isn't it beautiful?"

"Happy snow day, Hopper," Peter called.

Hopper **grunted**. He saw nothing happy about having to shovel.

Suddenly, his ears flew up with an idea. What if he got the kinderbunnies to shovel for him? After all, those **silly** little bunnies found fun in everything. They would **probably** even enjoy shoveling.

但是當這隻愛抱怨的小兔子一踏出門，他馬上被一群因為下雪而開心不已的兔寶寶們包圍。

小鬆餅笑著說，「是不是很漂亮呢？」

「波波，下雪天快樂，」彼得叫喊著。

波波埋怨地發出呼嚕聲。他實在看不出鏟雪有什麼值得高興的。

　　突然間，他把耳朵一豎，想到了個好主意。若是叫這些小兔子們幫他鏟雪呢？畢竟，那些小蠢蛋不論做什麼都能自得其樂。甚至，他們可能會覺得鏟雪很好玩呢！

Hopper turned to his students.

"Hot chocolate all around—if you shovel my walk," he proposed.

The kinderbunnies looked **skeptical**. "We can get hot chocolate at home without shoveling," Muffin pointed out.

Peter thought for a moment, then he smiled at Hopper. "We'll shovel your walk, *if* you take us **sledding** down the Big Hill first."

波波轉身走向他的學生們。「如果你們替我鏟雪，我就請你們每個人喝熱巧克力，」他提議著。小兔寶寶們滿臉狐疑。「我們不用鏟雪也可以在家裡喝到熱巧克力，」小鬆餅一語道破。彼得想了一會兒，然後笑著對波波說，「如果你先帶我們坐雪橇從比格山上滑下來的話，我們就替你鏟雪。」

"I don't know," **muttered** Hopper. "That doesn't sound like such a good idea to me."

"Please!" said all the kinderbunnies together. "Pretty please with **marshmallows** on top!"

"Oh, all right," Hopper grumped. "Let's get this over with." He and the kinderbunnies **tramped** through the **sparkling** snow to the Big Hill.

「我不曉得，」波波嘀咕著，「這聽起來似乎不是個好主意。」

「拜託啦！」所有的小兔寶寶都一起求他，「求求你帶我們到鋪滿雪棉糖的山頂上去嘛！」

「唉，好吧，」波波嘀咕著。「我們把這件事解決掉吧。」他和這些小兔寶寶們穿過閃閃發亮的皚皚白雪，來到了比格山。

"Okay, hurry up and have fun!"
Hopper **announced** when they reached the top of the Big Hill.
"We won't be here long!"

But no one was listening. The kinderbunnies were already sledding
down the long, **steep** hill, **squealing** with **glee**.

他們爬到比格山頂後，波波便發號施令，「好了，趕快去玩吧！我們不會在這兒待很久的！」
但是根本沒有人在聽他說話，小兔寶寶們早就從長長的陡陂上滑了下去，還一邊興奮地
尖叫著。

Hopper watched their first few runs. None of the bunnies was going as far or as fast as he knew he could.

He reached for Peter's sled. "Here, let me show you the right way to do it," he said.

Hopper ran as fast as he could, then **flopped** onto the sled. Soon he was **whooshing** full-speed down the Big Hill.

波波望著他們剛開始滑的樣子，沒有一隻兔寶寶可以像他一樣滑得又快又遠。

他走近彼得的雪橇說，「看著，讓你們瞧瞧真正的滑行方式。」

波波全力飛奔，然後縱身躍上了雪橇，一下子就以全速從比格山上咻咻地滑了下去。

By the time Hopper saw the **snowdrift**, it was too late. He **wiped** out in a **cascade** of **powdery** snow. It was wonderful!

等波波看到凸起的小雪堆時，已經來不及了。他拍掉身上大片大片粉末狀的雪花，這真是太有趣了！

Hopper couldn't wait to go again. As he pulled the
sled back up the hill, his ears **bounced merrily** with
each step.

　　波波等不及要再試一次。他把雪橇拉回山丘頂，兩隻長耳朵隨著每一次的步伐而愉悅地
彈跳著。

Finally, everyone was all **tuckered** out. "Let's go shovel the walk now," said Hopper, and all the kinderbunnies agreed.

But on the **shortcut** back to Hopper's house, the group passed a **frozen pond**.

最後，每個人都累了。「我們回去鏟雪吧，」波波說。所有的兔寶寶都同意了。
但是當他們走在回程的捷徑上時，他們經過一個結了冰的小池塘。

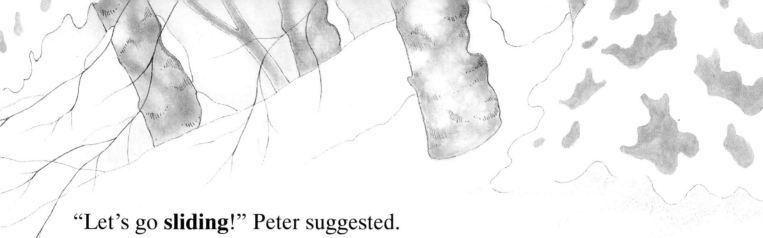

"Let's go **sliding**!" Peter suggested.

"Please, please, please!" the other kinderbunnies **chorused**.

Hopper glanced at the pond's **smooth**, shiny surface. It *did* look **tempting**. "I suppose it's my **duty** as a teacher to show you the proper way to slide," he offered.

The kinderbunnies **cheered**.

「我們來溜冰吧！」彼得建議。

「拜託！拜託！好不好嘛！」其他的兔寶寶都異口同聲地附和著。

波波看了看光滑如鏡的湖面，那的確很誘人。「我想，示範正確的溜冰方法是我當老師的職責，」他說。小兔寶寶們都歡呼了起來。

Hopper got a running start. When he had **picked up** enough speed, he jumped onto the ice and slid. The world **rushed** past him in a **blur** of **shimmering** snow. For a moment, he felt as if he were flying!

波波先助跑一段距離，等到速度夠了的時候，便一躍跳上冰面，開始溜了起來。整個世界都從他身旁呼嘯而過，他只能感覺到一陣模糊閃亮的雪光。有一會兒，波波還以為自己正在飛翔哩！

Then his foot hit a rock poking up through the ice. Hopper stuck
out his arms, **wiggled** his ears, and recovered his **balance**. "I've still
got it!" he cried **triumphantly** as he—

然後他的腳撞到了突出於冰層上的一塊小石塊，波波擺動雙臂，晃動著耳朵，又恢復了
平衡。「看我還是滑得那麼好！」他發出了勝利的呼聲—

哎喲——碰！波波隔著尾巴感覺到又硬又涼的冰塊。當他停下來時，聽到一陣滑稽的聲音，
咻——咻——咻！……碰，碰，碰！

FA-WHUMP! Hopper felt hard, cold ice under his tail.

As he **skidded** to a stop, he heard a funny sound: *FA-FA-FA...WHUMP, WHUMP, WHUMP!*

The kinderbunnies who had been sliding behind Hopper **tumbled** into one another like falling **dominoes**.

Flopsy laughed, and everyone joined in—even Hopper!

跟在波波身後溜著的小兔寶寶們一個接著一個地滑倒在一塊，就好像推倒的骨牌一樣。
晃晃笑了起來，然後大家都笑了起來──連波波也是。

這群兔寶寶離開了池塘，開始走回波波的房子，但是四周積得好深的白雪實在太誘人了。
「我們來玩雪球大戰！」小鬆餅高聲地叫。其他的兔寶寶們馬上衝向大雪堆，開始建造他
們的城堡。波波已經把鏟雪的事忘得一乾二淨。他愛死了雪球大戰！

The group left the pond and began to walk back to Hopper's house. But all that deep white snow was just too **enticing**.

"Let's have a snowball fight!" Muffin shouted.

The other bunnies ran to a big drift to build their **forts**.

Hopper forgot all about shoveling. He loved snowball fights!

The grumpy bunny cleared his **throat**. "I suppose I *should* teach you the right way to build a snow fort."

He showed the kinderbunnies how to shape mounds of snow into **sturdy shelters**.

這隻老愛發牢騷的兔子清了清喉嚨說，「我想我應該好好教你們用雪來堆城堡的正確方法。」他向這些小兔寶寶們示範了如何用一堆一堆的雪築成堅固的掩蔽物。

After Hopper and the kinderbunnies had built their forts, he taught them how to pack a perfect snowball.

Soon the bunnies were caught up in a **fierce** battle. Snowballs **whizzed** through the air. Bunnies from one fort tried to **sneak** up on the other. Walls were **battered** and rebuilt. Targets were **bombarded**. Mittens were **soaked**.

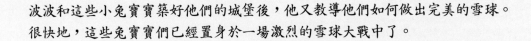

波波和這些小兔寶寶築好他們的城堡後，他又教導他們如何做出完美的雪球。
很快地，這些兔寶寶們已經置身於一場激烈的雪球大戰中了。

　　雪球在空中咻咻地飛來飛去，兩邊的兔寶寶都想要潛入對方的陣地中，雪牆被轟垮後又
再次重建了起來，目標物被轟炸了，手套也都溼透了。

Two kinderbunnies **grabbed** big round snowballs and came running at Hopper.

"Watch this **dodge**," he said, **diving** to one side.

Suddenly, he found himself staring up at the sky. Hopper had fallen backward onto the soft snow.

兩隻小兔寶寶突然抓起大顆的雪球向波波這兒跑來,「看我怎麼躲,」波波叫著跳向一旁。突然間,他發現他自己仰望著天空。波波四腳朝天跌坐在柔軟的雪堆裡。

He waved his arms up and down and **scissored** his legs in and out.

"Snow angels!" the kinderbunnies **exclaimed**. They all fell down in the snow and joined in.

Hopper and the kinderbunnies made snow angels all the way back to Hopper's house.

他躺在雪堆上揮舞著雙手和雙腳。

「白雪天使！」小兔寶寶們大聲叫喊著，紛紛跳入雪堆中和他一起躺著。

波波和小兔寶寶們就這樣一路玩著白雪天使的遊戲回波波家去。

"Now it really is time for shoveling," Hopper **declared**.
With all the kinderbunnies **pitching in**, shoveling wasn't boring at
all. In fact, Hopper had to **admit**—it was fun!

「真的是到了該鏟雪的時候了，」波波宣布著。
所有的兔寶寶都全心投注，鏟雪一點也不枯燥。事實上，波波不得不承認——那蠻有趣的！

First, they had a speed-shoveling race. Then there was a **contest** to see who could throw snow the highest and who could pitch it the farthest.

首先，他們先玩個快速鏟雪賽跑，接著比賽誰能將雪鏟得最高且丟得最遠。

Once all the snow was in a **giant heap**, Hopper looked
at it and had a wonderful thought. "Let's build a
snowbunny!"

The kinderbunnies were happy to help.

等到雪堆成了巨大的雪堆後，波波望著雪堆，心中浮現了一個很棒的主意，「我們來堆雪人！」

小兔寶寶們都興高采烈地幫忙。

In no time at all, the **spectacular statue** was done. But something was missing. "I think he needs some friends," Hopper suggested.

The bunnies worked quickly, and soon the big snowbunny was surrounded by lots of little snowbunnies. Hopper grinned. "That's much better."

幾乎沒有花什麼時間，這座醒目的雪兔塑像就完成了，但是還缺了點什麼。「我想它需要一些朋友，」波波提議著。

這些兔寶寶們很快地堆著雪，不一會兒，這隻大雪兔旁邊就圍繞了許多小雪兔。波波露出牙齒開心地笑著說，「這樣好多了。」

"I sure hope it snows tomorrow!" Daisy said.

"Me, too!" Flopsy cried. "Me, three!" the other bunnies cheered.

And **to his amazement**, Hopper agreed. "I have an idea," he said.

"Let's do a snowdance." Peter was confused. "A snowdance?"

"You know—like a raindance, only for snow," Flopsy explained.

「我真希望明天也下雪！」黛西說。「我也希望！」晃晃叫喊著。

「我們也是！」其他的兔寶寶們也雀躍地回應著。而令波波感到訝異的是，他自己也希望明天下雪。「我有個主意，」他說，「我們來跳雪舞。」彼得不懂他的意思，「跳雪舞？」「你知道的——就像祈雨的舞蹈一樣，只是我們要祈求下雪，」晃晃解釋著。

But Hopper had already begun. He **weaved** between the snow-covered trees, throwing his head back to look at the sky.

They danced till they were **dizzy** and all the parents throughout the woods started calling the kinderbunnies to come home.

但是波波已經開始跳了起來，他在被雪覆蓋的大樹中間鑽來穿去，不時抬起頭仰望天空。

他們跳得暈頭轉向，一直到森林中所有兔寶寶的爸爸媽媽們開始呼喚孩子回家時為止。

"Thanks for a wonderful day!" the kinderbunnies said as they hopped away. "Thank *you!*" said Hopper.

And as he watched them leave, Hopper remembered a **rhyme** he'd learned back when *he* was a kinderbunny at Easter Bunny Elementary School:

> *No matter what the weather brings,*
> *an Easter Bunny makes it spring.*
> *Find sunshine in every day —*
> *That's the Easter Bunny way!*

兔寶寶們蹦蹦跳跳地離開了，他們不忘對波波說，「謝謝您給我們這麼美好的一天！」
「也謝謝你們！」波波說。看著他們離開，波波回想起當他在就讀復活節兔寶寶小學時，學到的一首童謠：
不管颱風或下雪，復活節兔寶寶讓它變春天。
陽光每天笑臉來──復活節兔寶寶永不改變。

cheer [tʃɪr] 　動 歡呼

chorus [`korəs] 　動 異口同聲

contest [`kɑntɛst] 　名 比賽

admit [əd`mɪt] 　動 承認

announce [ə`naʊns] 　動 宣布

declare [dɪ`klɛr] 　動 宣告

dive [daɪv] 　動 潛跳

dizzy [`dɪzɪ] 　形 頭暈的

dodge [dɑdʒ] 　名 閃躲

domino [`dɑmə,no] 　名 骨牌

due to 　由於

duty [`djutɪ] 　名 責任

balance [`bæləns] 　名 平衡

batter [`bætɚ] 　動 連續地重擊

blur [blɝ] 　名 朦朧

bombard [bɑm`bɑrd] 　動 砲擊，轟炸

boot [but] 　名 靴子

bother [`bɑðɚ] 　名 麻煩

bounce [baʊns] 　動 彈跳

bunch [bʌntʃ] 　名 一群

enticing [ɪn`taɪsɪŋ] 　形 誘人的

exclaim [ɪk`sklem] 　動 叫喊

cascade [kæs`ked] 　名 瀑布

fierce [fɪrs]　形　猛烈的

flop [flɑp]　動　突然倒下

fort [fort]　名　堡壘

frozen [`frozn̩]　形　結冰的

fuss [fʌs]　名　無謂的紛擾

giant [`dʒaɪənt]　形　巨大的

glee [gli]　名　喜悅

grab [græb]　動　抓

grumble [`grʌmbl̩]　動　抱怨

grumpy [`grʌmpɪ]　形　愛抱怨的

grunt [grʌnt]　動　發出咕嚕聲

heap [hip]　名　堆積

marshmallow [`marʃ,mælo]　名　雪棉糖

merrily [`mɛrɪlɪ]　副　愉悅地

mitten [`mɪtn̩]　名　（僅姆指分開）連指手套

mutter [`mʌtɚ]　動　喃喃自語

pester [`pɛstɚ]　動　使……煩惱

pick up　加快（速度）

pitch in　努力合作

pond [pɑnd]　名　池塘

powdery [`paʊdərɪ]　形　粉狀的

probably [`prɑbəblɪ]　副　或許

relief [rɪ`lif]　名　放心

rhyme [raɪm]　名　押韻詩

rush [rʌʃ]　動　急奔

surround [sə`raʊnd]　動 包圍

S

scarf [skɑrf]　名 圍巾

scissor [`sɪzɚ]　動 剪

shelter [`ʃɛltɚ]　名 庇護所

shimmering [`ʃɪmərɪŋ]　形 閃爍的

shortcut [`ʃɔrt,kʌt]　名 捷徑

shovel [`ʃʌvl̩]　動 用鏟子鏟……

sigh [saɪ]　動 嘆氣

silly [`sɪlɪ]　形 愚蠢的

skeptical [`skɛptɪkl̩]　形 疑惑的

skid [skɪd]　動 打滑

sled [slɛd]　動 滑雪橇

slide [slaɪd]　動 溜冰

smooth [smuð]　形 平滑的

sneak [snik]　動 偷偷接近

snowdrift [`sno,drɪft]　名 雪堆

soak [sok]　動 浸溼

sparkling [`sparklɪŋ]　形 閃耀的

spectacular [spɛk`tækjəlɚ]　形 壯觀的

squeal [skwil]　動 尖叫

statue [`stætʃʊ]　名 雕像

steep [stip]　形 陡峭的

sturdy [`stɝdɪ]　形 堅固的

T

tempting [`tɛmptɪŋ]　形 誘人的

throat [θrot]　名 喉嚨

to one's amazement　令……驚訝的是

tramp [træmp]　動 拖著沈重的腳步走

triumphantly [traɪ`ʌmfəntlɪ]　副 得意洋洋地

tucker [`tʌkɚ]　動 使疲倦 《out》

tumble [`tʌmbl̩]　動 摔倒

W

weave [wiv]　動 穿梭

whiz [hwɪz]　動 咻咻地飛

whoosh [hwuʃ]　動 發出咻咻聲

wiggle [`wɪgl̩]　動 晃動

wipe [waɪp]　動 擦去

個兒不高・志氣不小・智勇雙全・人人叫好

我是大喜，
別看我個兒小小，

我可是把兇惡的噴火龍耍得團團轉！
連最狡滑的巫婆也大呼受不了呢！
想知道我這些有趣的冒險故事嗎？

探索英文叢書・中高級
Upper Intermediate

中英對照

● 大 喜 說 故 事 系 列 ●

Anna Fienberg & Barbara Fienberg／著

Kim Gamble／繪　王秋瑩／譯

每本均附CD

（本系列陸續出版中）

國家圖書館出版品預行編目資料

波波的下雪天 / Justine Korman著;Lucinda McQueen
繪;[三民書局]編輯部譯.--初版一刷.--臺北
市;三民，民90
　　面;公分--(探索英文叢書.波波唸翻天系列;5)
中英對照
ISBN 957-14-3444-2　(平裝)

1.英國語言—讀本

805.18　　　　　　　　　　　　　　90003948

網路書店位址　http://www.sanmin.com.tw

© 　波波的下雪天

著作人　Justine Korman
繪　圖　Lucinda McQueen
譯　者　三民書局編輯部
發行人　劉振強
著作財
產權人　三民書局股份有限公司
　　　　臺北市復興北路三八六號
發行所　三民書局股份有限公司
　　　　地址／臺北市復興北路三八六號
　　　　電話／二五○○六六○○
　　　　郵撥／○○○九九九八──五號
印刷所　三民書局股份有限公司
門市部　復北店／臺北市復興北路三八六號
　　　　重南店／臺北市重慶南路一段六十一號
初版一刷　中華民國九十年四月
編　號　S 85593
定　價　新臺幣壹佰捌拾元
行政院新聞局登記證局版臺業字第○二○○號

ISBN　957-14-3444-2　(平裝)

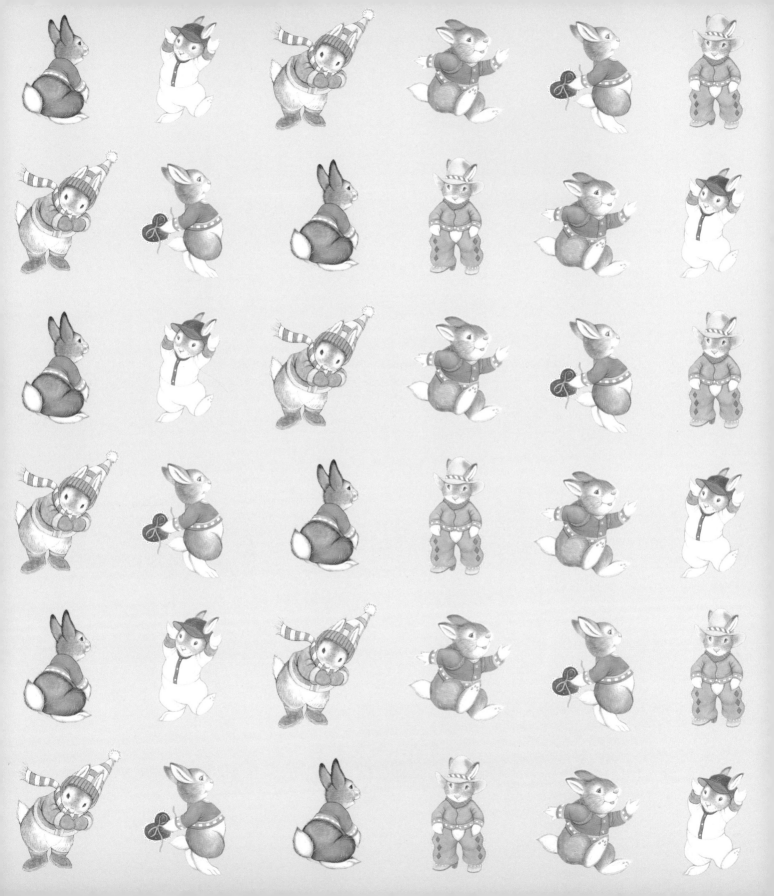

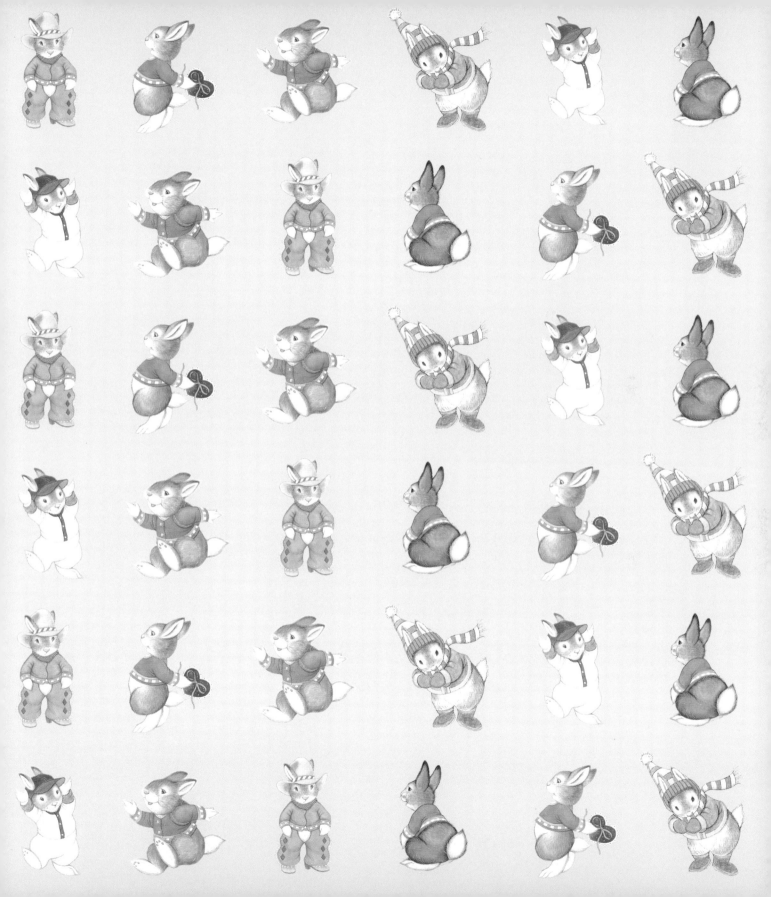